"In *Echo Chamber*, Claire Hopple's precise, shimmering sentences are on full display as she explores the inner workings of these unforgettable characters. Once I started reading this book, I couldn't put it down. It's a refreshing, innovative collection."

  —Chelsea Hodson, author of *Tonight I'm Someone Else*

"Claire Hopple writes like she's planning a bank robbery on acid, only the bank is a hot air balloon, and there's no such thing as money. Part Amelia Gray, part Mary Robison, part love letter to the subconscious, *Echo Chamber* will steal your identity and leave you profoundly, delightfully awake."

  —Kevin Maloney, author of *The Red-Headed Pilgrim*

"Echo Chamber is sharp, wry, wicked fun. Claire Hopple has a light, humorous touch, but there's no question she means business."

  —Lindsay Lerman, author of *What Are You?*

"Acerbic, observant and wise, Claire Hopple makes magic with the flash epistolary form, translating the experimental into an emotionally affecting, lovely book."

  —Chaya Bhuvaneswar, author of *White Dancing Elephants*, a PEN/American Bingham Prize finalist.

"Claire Hopple writes with such concision and style, I had to scrape my jaw from the floor after reading. It's hard to say just how good this little book truly is without sounding hyperbolic, but I'll try. It is great."

  —Troy James Weaver, author of *Temporal*

TAKE IT PERSONALLY

ALSO BY CLAIRE HOPPLE

Echo Chamber

It's Hard to Say

Tell Me How You Really Feel

Tired People Seeing America

Too Much of the Wrong Thing

CLAIRE HOPPLE

TAKE IT PERSONALLY

STALKING HORSE PRESS
SANTA FE, NEW MEXICO

CONTENTS...

PART I

...CONTENTS

PART II

PART III

Oh, what will I do when nothing happens to me?
—My Morning Jacket

…you found a plenitude of remnants: fragments of our living,
tiny novels, small fires.
—Renee Gladman

What doesn't need glue?
—Mary Robison

TAKE IT PERSONALLY

PART 1

1

THE CAGE OF YOUR OWN PERSONALITY

UNBEKNOWNST TO EVERYONE, I am hired to follow a famous diarist. My objective is simple: Determine whether the initials in her published entries are thinly veiled names from her closest circles or altogether fabricated characters. To see whether these secret—now not-so-secret—trysts and assignations are the result of a life lived vigorously, or a life lived entirely within the realm of the mind. I'm not sure which is worse. But my feelings aren't supposed to be included in the assignment anyway.

Most days I follow her around a manmade lake named after a colonizer.

My employers have not fully revealed themselves. I ask for details, but they say I'm not prepared for them. Who knows how they found me. They might have chosen me simply because I live a block and a half away from this famous diarist. Sometimes it's nice to aimlessly adhere to a minor celebrity within an operation designed at the whim of specialists. I'm flattered to coagulate in the seedy murk of encounters typically left to the retirees that compose our neighborhood watch.

Is her husband luring striper or stripper into his pontoon boat? Is she? It's all up in the air. There is no plan. Or the plan is unburdened by itinerary. You can't make a plan when you follow someone—that's the antithesis of following. I may be new at this but I'm not dumb. You trail and you steep in another's decisions. You are freed from the cage of your own personality. That is until your snack bag runs low or your legs cramp or your eyes cloud over from literal pond scum (manmade lake scum?) and seasonal weeds. I wobble along her orbit and then eventually I return to myself.

As luck would have it, Bianca the diarist lives directly beside the neighbor who's always had the hots for me. The guy who does all his leaf blowing in the nude. When people stare, he tells them not to worry about it. Oh, Bruce, you rascal. The only house on the street with underage kids installed blackout curtains and an aggressive row of shrubbery.

When I think about it, I haven't seen Bruce lately. Maybe he really got busted this time.

Going through this rigmarole and actually getting paid for it—assuming it's not rigged somehow, an elaborate setup—you could call it a chance to gather myself. After being usurped at the office by a doe-eyed 20-something who wears heels on purpose, you could say this is an essential encounter that will supplement my paid gigs at the local clubs. That's right, I'm the lead singer of Rhonda & the Sandwich Artists. You've probably heard of us. In a sense, it's like celebrity-tailing-celebrity here. I write my own lyrics. We're at the cusp of fame. We're cusping pretty hard, if you can believe it.

At least this job is better than sitting on my cracked back patio pretending to apply to freelance copywriting positions while staring at the sinkhole underneath the gazebo.

At night, I study the only image of Bianca and me together, although she probably wouldn't even recognize me now. It's nestled in an old neighborhood newsletter. We're with a group of 30 or so holding up those violent sticks used to clear litter, trying not to side-eye the people adjacent who might or might not have been a little unwieldy with their tools. I think Bianca even proofread this periodical at one point, before she got really big, which is more than I ever do around here.

This isn't even what a real investigation is like. But I'm accumulating unexpected self-improvements, like how to wave my hair the right way or what potions women like me are supposed to put on their faces at night. Snooping both amplifies and dissolves my ignorance, it turns out. I'm learning things as if I planned it all along.

I've started cataloging her habits in ways that aren't entirely helpful. Crayon renderings, haikus, lists.

What she doesn't use: her saltwater hot tub, her outdoor chimney complete with pizza oven rack, her robot vacuum, her easy path to the neighborhood market with hand-painted cartoon tomatoes on the sign.

What she uses with regularity: her sunglasses, her stretch pants, her lipstick, her name.

"S" marks the spot. Her serpentine first floor is where she spends most of her time. She'll make these elaborate breakfasts that nobody touches, and I wonder if it's a trap. The waffle maker as a form of misdirection.

There's no way of knowing, but before long, I could become a sensation. I've always preferred and sought after invisibility. Remaining invisible is what I'm best at. That's probably why I haven't been caught spying yet. I'm so good, in fact, that sometimes I get sick of it. And in those times, I wish I played the tuba. Because you can't ignore a tuba. In other moments, I never want to be noticed or receive attention ever again.

Emailing reports to my employers, I feel something that could be considered 'belonging.'

I didn't turn them down. I haven't sabotaged any of my own efforts so far. That is a start.

2

POPCORN

I MEET A guy named Popcorn sitting outside the neighborhood market.

"Tell me, if you were a detective, how would you infiltrate the suspect's home without breaking and entering or any of that technically illegal stuff?" I ask him.

"I would get a warrant," he says.

"And what if you couldn't get a warrant?"

"Who wants to know, anyway?"

"It's for a school project," I say.

"A school project? How old are you?" Popcorn says.

"Doesn't matter."

Popcorn goes on to advise me that the best course of action is to pretend I'm selling solar panels. He watches without comment as a TV crew filters in and out of a news van. Bruce still hasn't come back. The crew has arrived because he's officially been reported missing.

I'm here to get out of the house. Bunking with a self-proclaimed psychic takes its toll. Especially in an unassuming suburb embroiled in single-family homes. I rented it for the secret passageway. Turns out the rest of it is junk. I can do a lot with a secret passageway though. As is my custom.

Do I have what it takes to become a solar panel professional? I want to purchase a walkie talkie but then I remember this is a one-way operation. Maybe I'll just browse some options on the internet. You never know.

Popcorn's still absorbing the debacle before us. He's unimpressed, I can tell. He seems like the type who maintains order around here. I consider telling him that a reliable source from the neighborhood watch—I always forget her name… Marjorie? Sheryl maybe—stated Bruce was last seen at the roller disco he owned. But Popcorn's probably already acquired this information if I have. So I settle for a wave goodbye.

As I walk away, he says, "You don't need to lie to me."

3

THE NEXT BIG THING

HERE WE ARE. In Bianca's house. I didn't even need to take Popcorn's advice (though I would no doubt make a passable solar panel expert) because Bianca posted about a painting for sale.

That's a gimme if I've ever seen one. The painting is vaporous and vaguely geometric, but her post says it's supposed to represent the city dump. I don't know what to make of it.

Bianca doesn't recognize me as a neighbor, just as I assumed.

"I'm Tori. I live a block and a half away," I say, smiling.

Maybe I should've used a fake name. Too late now.

"Oh, really?"

"I can present credentials."

"That won't be necessary."

I look out her window and say, "Do you think there'll be an uprising?"

"What for?"

"You know, this Bruce business."

"Liz told me he was caught storing a high volume of dynamite in his basement. As far as the police department's concerned, he's a person of interest."

Liz. That's the hotshot from neighborhood watch. Not Marjorie. And there's never even been a resident named Sheryl since I've lived here, now that I think about it.

"I hadn't heard that."

"Liz's constituents are handing out informational leaflets at the corner all the time," Bianca says.

An actual private investigator would have managed to gather these leaflets in advance. What can you do?

"You know, Bruce was in the neighborhood watch decades ago. Back in the days of their all-you-can-eat buffets."

"Huh. I can't even picture that," I say.

She goes upstairs to retrieve the painting. I briefly consider rifling through her drawers, but then confront the reality of my poor reaction time. I could take this mission and run it right into the ground.

Bianca immediately returns. She passes off the monstrosity in a gilt frame. "We have a Noah Verrier original now," she says.

The painting's heavy, and all the questions I've prepared have disappeared, so I leave.

Nobody tells me Bruce's roller disco is frequented by the nephew of a former dictator of Nicaragua. They supposedly own a racetrack together in the town beside us too, but its existence is disputed, according to my research. And from what I collect on another fact-finding quest, there's no private investigator handbook that's free and open to the public.

Bruce is maybe trying to make a point to someone

somewhere, and it may or may not be getting across, but his point is crucial to a particular way he wants life to be.

My reports thus far aren't encouraging. These emails to my employer are forming into a thicket of hearsay. They've become a platform for my insecurities. Everyone's more knowledgeable than me, and they know it.

As if it matters, I hang Bianca's painting above my bed. I search for a clause in my contract that supplies me with cash for extraneous expenses, such as buying this painting. No such luck.

I'll get to the next big thing before anybody else. I'll crack the code of Bianca's public confessions and find time to save Bruce too. I've never been one to avoid grandiose delusions about myself and I'm not going to start now.

4

RESULTS

THERE ARE SO many things you can't say when you're undercover.

It all happens very fast. Bianca's husband gets flown home in a helicopter by one of his compatriots. They land beside the neighbor's strawberry patch.

He's returned promptly for his weekly appointment. Someone visits their house and rocks him like a baby for an hour every Wednesday like it's totally normal.

Just who is Ryan, anyway? Besides the spouse of a famous diarist, he's tangled in the barbarous realm of high finance. And his old trophies from various competitive eating championships commandeer their living room shelves. I saw so for myself when I picked up the painting.

Meanwhile somewhere above me—I can say that with slight confidence based on some general coordinates from scrounged IP addresses—atop one of our town's rolling hills, sit my employers. They're constructing a scaffolding of secrets based on my precious observations. And what would their next reaction be but one full of complaints. They say there's nothing to show for what I've done, just showmanship. That my emails are unremarkable. They insist I must produce results. My guess is they're disappointed in my last report describing illicit teeter-tottering at the park between Bianca and a presumed boyfriend, since they were literally using the teeter totter and not emotionally vacillating between continuing an affair or returning to their marriages. At least from what I could tell.

Regardless, I don't buy it. I'm invading privacy like nobody's business. I'm taking to every assignment. I'm plastering myself to the facts. Even more than all that, I'm cooperating. The only place I could see myself really improving is if my notes could self-destruct. Maybe they want me to self-destruct. But I remain. My personhood persists.

To calm down, I slosh around in the garage until I find a bifurcated red ribbon with "A+ Reader" in gold script. I tape it to my chest for the rest of the day. Negative feedback won't stand in my way, and neither will any required reading. A plus.

In the spirit of refocusing my efforts, I pull out one of Bianca's books and recite an excerpt aloud:

> *I can't forget the way they all ganged up on me last night at V's—V, the very woman whose dignity was in question—after the unspeakable truth came out. J was the least of her problems at that point. Everybody snoops around and rifles through everyone else's belongings, but as soon as you veer toward a nervous breakdown or a confrontation of any kind, then they all start paying attention. T dragged me upstairs. She soothed me to the extent that I neglected the task at hand. Little does she know that now I'll always be in her care.*

In a moment of weakness, I do the right thing. I figure out where to go next. I only indulge about five to ten minutes of daydreaming first, wondering if Ryan has fallen in love with me yet.

5

AS SEEN ON TV

"IS THIS UP for grabs?" I ask the waiter, gesturing toward the linen napkin in front of me and placing it in my doggy bag.

He recoils.

I concede, handing it to him.

"You can keep your luxury napkin."

I'm branching out, following members of Bianca's inner circle. That's probably the only way I'll get to the bottom of this.

In an approximation of milling about, I observe Bianca's friend Veronica—the supposed "V" in her entries—collude with someone who looks almost exactly like her.

They greet each other. Veronica points to herself and says, "As seen on TV."

They commit to what can only be called uproarious laughter.

The friend has brought along her Lhasa Apso named Tater Tot.

Between their second and third round of mimosas, the friend slides over a slip of paper. I spill my water so I can lean in close enough to peek. It's a list of addresses in New York,

Los Angeles, Chicago, Miami. I capture the list with my mental camera, but the photo comes out blurry in my imagination, and whatever negatives remain are buried in a mound of pruned synapses amid the cellar of my hippocampus.

A call comes in. It's a major opportunity. A chance to rock with the big boys.

I ask this guy if our band can have access to the green room. The one with the good snacks. There's a vague exhale of permission on the other end.

"Forget it. Either way, we're in."

Given the rest of Rhonda & the Sandwich Artists' known propensity to ignore all phone calls, I text them the news.

This venue's where the good Blockbuster used to be, right beside the WE CURE BALDNESS billboard along the edge of the cemetery. The ad almost touches a few of their gravestones.

I'll be honest: The real reason we get so many gigs around town isn't our natural musical ability like I said before. We get booked because we're tidy. We have a reputation for picking up after ourselves. We don't rage-smash instruments or equipment. We leave things, dare I say, better than we find them. Just as I leave my suspects to their beverages, food, and pets named after food.

Back at home, my roommate informs me someone's been depositing death threats into our mailbox. She won't let me see them. She thinks they'll agitate my infamous night terrors. I can't say I blame her.

There's still no word on Bruce. The news vans have long since packed up.

I caress the edges of that ancient neighborhood newsletter and stare into everyone's poorly printed eyes. I'm starting to wonder if our friendly neighborhood watch is more of a dastardly secret society. And perhaps they're not too pleased with my superior snooping skills. They've noticed, and now they're slinging threats as a series of diversions.

If so, they can't get away with it. But they probably will.

6

THE FUSS

LYING IN THE sinkhole beneath the gazebo, you swear you can feel it plunge itself further into the ground, seeping toward the core. Getting to the good stuff. You can find anything you're looking for in this sinkhole. Answers. Conspiracies. Abandoned gummy bears. Bottles of wine coolers that have been discontinued since the 90s. They all materialize.

"I can see you," my roommate Allison says.

"Don't look at me."

Dressing up in costume is typically frowned upon, with the exception of certain holidays and very specific contexts. And Allison's caught me here covered from ear to fake tail in tiger fur.

"I've always been here. I've been here since the beginning of time," I continue, maneuvering into an upright position. "I suppose I should be dressed in some kind of business suit. Would that make you happy?"

Her face gauzes over into a cultivated expression; one of disappointment or superiority, I'm unable to tell the difference.

I've borrowed the high school mascot outfit to stake out Friday's game. It only took a small bribe. Everybody will be there, and in my tiger disguise, I can spy with ease. Supervising the game'll be better than surrendering the night to Bruce's racetrack or the parched landscape of our historic drive-in theater. Still, I wish they'd chosen a mascot with a sword or a cloak.

I told my employers: I know my way around a football field. You don't have to worry. But if you want me to do this right, you'll need to fetch me a roll of ones and an industrial sized container of baby powder.

Bianca doesn't like meeting the expectations of others, so I doubt she'll be there. Or maybe she simply disregards those expectations altogether. I bet she doesn't trouble herself with any of it.

"You'd better come with me," Allison says.

"You're still here? Oh."

I follow her into the kitchen.

"There's a whirring sound. What is this thing, anyway?"

"It's a trash compactor. In the 80s, people demanded to have them installed in their lackluster homes to feel more modernized. I guess garbage was a lot fluffier then too. Torn shoulder pads. Permed wigs or some such. You must've just flicked a switch accidentally," I say, fumbling with buttons.

She arranges the forks in a line on the counter.

"And I have a question for you. Why do you use a lunchbox? You work from home."

"You're jealous. I can tell," she says.

"And what kind of psychic is named Allison?" I say to her retreating figure.

Before I know it, I'm lolling around the bleachers. And by

lolling around, I mean turning myself loose on all the grownups in matching colors. No secret will be left intact by the night's end.

A squadron of neighborhood watchers flank the chain link beside the snack bar, conducting experiments among themselves and holding bystanders responsible for who knows what.

One of them cradles what appears to be a treasure map, and I'm not sure if I should take it literally or draw a connection to the opposing team, which happens to bedeck itself in the attire of swashbucklers.

Liz—most likely their ringleader, as we've established—walks over.

"I know you're in there, Tori. This must be very embarrassing for you."

I feel embarrassed in a brand-new way. We have no prior dealings with one another. I always accept the neighborhood watch leaflets with exuberance now. I even consult them from time to time.

Liz loses interest while I'm thinking of how to respond.

The others accompany her to their seats while I go to work on the dollar hot dogs, untucking my roll of ones. Pumping every condiment available onto my dinner, I can sort of see what all the fuss is about with these extracurricular activities. I suppose you'd call it a sense of camaraderie.

I avoid Liz the rest of the night. You know, for her sake. Her kids have left for college already. What's she even doing here?

For my final act, I will turn a few cartwheels and stumble to my car.

Back at headquarters, I extract myself from my costume and start sewing one for Tater Tot. Nobody asked me to do this. He'd look quite handsome as a sailor though.

I hear the distinct growl of Ryan's car down the street and drop my yarn. I think he's coming over to ask me some personal questions, but it doesn't happen. He's returning home. The tension is undeniable, however, so I know it's only a matter of time before we announce to Bianca that we're moving to the countryside without her. There's a phenomenal plot of land out by the bus graveyard. His silence speaks volumes.

Seeing as it's also an opportunity for reconnaissance, I trail him and observe as he parks in their driveway. But instead of using the front door, he shimmies up the siding and grips the shingles of their lower roof.

You know how this goes. Marital strife in all likelihood. I guess Bianca could've accidentally locked him out. The first answer feels right. It just is.

Ryan pops open a window and glides across the threshold.

And then what. I wait. I stare at the bushes I'm hiding behind so thoroughly that I seriously consider the topiary arts. There's nothing holding me back.

7

EXIT STRATEGIES

NOW IT'S MORNING. The precise time our local network airs its live morning show. My left eye twitches from a night's stay in a tent beside the studio. Here I am, staking out the lot where Bianca will appear as a guest, when I realize it would've been better just to watch the show at home. I can't see anything.

Seems like camping should've helped somehow. I'll disregard these details in my report. That and me falling into a dumpster while seeking a superior vantage. I'm mingling with resignation and fraternizing with garbage. Yeah, I'm still in the dumpster. It's hard to get out, okay?

I thought Bianca would be surrounded by admirers to theatrical effect, a swarm assembling outside the studio with posters bedecked in puffy paint, sandwiching themselves between fire lanes and the wall of windows fronting the lobby. No fanfare is being bandied about, as far as I can tell. Not even a smattering. Color me perplexed.

Almost as confounding as my conversation with Allison last night, which went like this:

"Good luck on your expedition," she said.

"What? You're not supposed to know about that."

"Then quit leaving your laptop in the bathroom," she said.

Ah, the bathroom. That old familiar place.

"Here, I made you this."

She handed me a briefcase. I popped it open. It was filled with Little Debbies of every variety. Quite a specimen, really. I could maneuver about the city with stockpiles like this.

Then she said, "You're staring."

"I'm trying to send you a message."

"I'm part of the psychic network, not telepathic."

"I'm not responsible for parsing out your exploits," I said.

"Probably a good thing you're headed out. We've received more death threats."

I collected my valuables.

"Many more," she added.

And now my hours in this lot are numbered. I emerge from the dumpster with what can only be described as ferocity.

I deduce that Trish is probably here too. Trish the assistant. Bianca's new assistant. Though Bianca prefers the term "associate." We all know that Trish is really her handler. One needs to rely on a tireless handler if one wants to give the appearance of independence. Trish is a steady person, which imbues her with mystery to me.

As I'm about to open the briefcase filled with Little Debbies for my private consumption, this guy opens the studio door and beckons me over. I'm the closest thing to a person within sight, so I fasten myself to whatever his identity for me might be. An opening for the taking.

"You must be our AC lifesaver. Even our cameras are sweating."

I look down. I'm wearing a gray jumpsuit.

"Ah, yes. My workman's attire. This isn't a disguise."

He ushers me into the lobby. It exudes the characteristic embellishments of a suburban office park.

"I'll give you a few seconds to admire the space before we continue," he says. "Where are my manners? Would you like a glass of water before you get started?"

"No, thank you. I'm made mostly of water. I'm watered down."

We climb some stairs.

"We have a hula hooping celebrity fitness instructor on tomorrow, so it's crucial that we get this squared away. Then the author of The Owner's Manual for Stomachs is on Thursday. I'm really looking forward to that one."

He keeps turning around to gauge my reaction every few seconds and I almost ram into him each time. But if masquerading were easy then everybody would do it.

"Our thousands of viewers don't tune in for the flashy spectacles though. They show up for the psychological wounds. The eviscerating destruction of our civilization," he continues.

"Um."

We amble down a long hallway until we reach what looks to be a dressing room.

"Here we go. The AC unit's over on that far wall."

He opens a closet door with a series of identical outfits lined up in a row like it's a cartoon character's wardrobe.

I turn away in case he's about to change. I'm an amateur spy, not a pervert.

"My tools," I say, feeling along the edge of my hips as if they could be lodged there, "Must've left them in the truck."

"Not a problem. Happens to the best of us. We do have some in the utility room if you'd prefer."

Before I can respond he's out the door. He returns with an oversized toolbox.

"Ooh, look. There's a sledgehammer in here," he says.

He grabs the sledgehammer and says some words I'd rather not repeat. Then he starts wailing away on the paisley print sofa with ruffle trim in the corner of the room. He really gets after it. Splinters are being forged right in front of our eyes.

He runs out of breath. The sledgehammer clatters onto the floor.

"It's fine," he says between heaves. "I own this place. Really. Signed the papers yesterday."

I concede my shocked expression. Still, I take it upon myself to concoct a list of exit strategies. It goes without saying that anything left unrebutted from this job will go in my tell-all.

A ruffled seam floats down next to the sledgehammer as if it's confronting him.

"On Friday, we'll cover the latest investigative report about a robber breaking into a locksmith's house. Our viewers love irony."

I smile. I only smile when I'm uncomfortable.

"Anyway, he's dead now."

I do not ask if he means the robber or the locksmith, or any other information that might make me an accomplice later on.

Sidling past him, I mutter something about a special air conditioning tool in the truck.

I escape in time to witness Bianca power-walking to her car with Trish in tow. Bianca drops a slip of paper. Neither one of them notice.

I scoop it up and pocket it, but I can already tell without actually reading it that it's a grocery list.

Bianca. I'm constantly surprised by what she'll make me say and do, especially since we don't really interact. I'm mimicking her voice and her head shake and her leg fidgets, and I'm aware of this, but I keep doing it. My aping is insufficient. She lords over me like the neighborhood watch lords over our quaint municipality. Which is exactly what I'll infiltrate next.

8

WHAT'S WHAT

IF YOU BELIEVE in sandwich rings like I do, the choice is clear: You must attend the neighborhood watch meeting. Sandwich rings are one of only about five things I believe in. An endless circle of bread that puts the "deli" in "delicious." They procure at least one every meeting, or so I'm told. That next sandwich ring holds a lot of information about my fate and the safety of this very neighborhood. I need to see what's what. Figure out where these death threats are coming from.

Popcorn's out in front of the market again.

I ask him, "How does one go about joining the neighborhood watch?"

"Heh. They've been trying to recruit me for years."

"So you need an invitation."

"Something like that."

I've never had much luck with groupthink. Never been part of an association or club of any sort.

"How might—"

"—We'll need beverages to answer that," Popcorn interrupts, motioning toward the market.

I buy some drinks and grab the brand of granola bars from Bianca's found grocery list. Soon the oatmeal will linger in my molars.

I hand Popcorn the goods. He tells me his findings, a rather complete dossier on the seemingly prehistoric gathering of neighbors. Most of it is over my head. I space out for a few minutes, completely missing the best parts.

As a kind of goodbye, he says, "You might want to get a haircut first."

On the corner, a kid's waiting for the bus with a field trip itinerary in his little mitts. I approach him and say, "It's no different when you're older."

Once I return home, Allison's not there to give me a free haircut, so I steal a hat from her closet that makes me look more interesting. I adjust the brim with great pomp.

The watch meets at dusk in an unmarked municipal building. It's likely some annex of our migratory police department.

No droning chants emanate from behind the door. And no cloaks adorn its members once I peek through a seam. Do they at least give you a discount at the Tire Depot? Triple-A offers me that much.

Neighborhood watchers huddle at the room's entrance with the inelegance of the highly organized. They'd repel prospective members if they hadn't acquired so much leverage, mostly in the form of town memorabilia, personal property, and open secrets.

Pam with the cloth headband stands behind a welcome table. Her partless hair is gently swooped back behind a swath of polka dot.

"Give me the very best name tag you have," I say to her.

"Oh, hey, Tori," she says.

"I need one for sentimental purposes. An emotional support name tag."

Pam lives right next door to us. She'll often knock right after my self-administered sessions of scream therapy.

"I'll just give you a blank one to fill out," Pam says, as if her statement is supported by kindness.

"I want to blend in. I mean, I want to serve our community."

Liz addresses the crowd with an intern taking notes by her side. She almost tramples him attempting to usher everyone into their seats.

As a last-ditch effort, I whisper to Pam, "Let's trade name tags. Live each other's lives for a while. See if anyone can tell the difference."

She smiles and adjusts the fresh tag on my bosom.

I swipe a Sharpie and autograph a corner of the welcome table while she's looking the other way.

In this hat, I could be anyone. These people could all be seeking my counsel.

"There she is," Liz says from the front. "Our special guest, Tori."

I think maybe Liz is trying to trick me. Folks look over their shoulders halfheartedly and applaud.

"Now, Darren, according to the logbook, what's our first agenda item?" Liz asks from behind a podium that's somehow materialized.

The intern clears his throat and says, "The pack of street dogs."

"Who needs animal control when we have Bruce," shouts someone from the chairs.

The room falls silent. Bruce is still missing. Though rumors have been piling up about him getting detained at the border.

"Moving along," says Liz, "We have the trash bin debacle. People are getting confused about the bin colors and dumping perfectly good recyclable material into the wrong place."

I raise my hand, remember this isn't school, and emphatically slam my knuckles back into my lap.

"The bin situation is uncalled for. We all know Larry is colorblind too. These things need to be clearly marked."

A few attendees nod. I feed off their mild enthusiasm.

"And furthermore, they need to be power-washed every quarter by this enterprising young intern of yours."

I swear Liz's eyes turn into gavels for about three seconds. Before I know it, I'm handed a meeting agenda that says SEE ME AFTER.

In moments like these you can be hopeful and assume someone's going to fill you in on the dangers looming in your mailbox, or you can prepare for the worst: total banishment from the neighborhood watch, and perhaps, the neighborhood altogether.

Then Darren has a firm grasp on my shoulder. "Say goodbye now," he says.

He's much stronger than he appears. He points to the autographed table.

"Who can explain it?" I say.

"Well, autographing is still participating in a lot of ways," says Pam.

"Pam. Sweet Pam. Take me with you."

We'd rediscover the sonic stylings of Christopher Cross. She'd teach me how to tie my shoes the more traditional way. I'd forget the bunny ears method entirely. My life would be grander but somehow less terrifying, much like I imagine Bianca's life to be.

Before I know it, I'm at my car. I'm staring into the driver's side door at my own reflection, literally beside myself. The meeting agenda is tucked neatly into my cupholder. Darren's a paper enthusiast; I should've spotted it right away.

"You can keep it," he shouts from the door, then scuttles back inside.

As they busy themselves with paltry affairs and the intern overstays his welcome, I'm struck with an observation that could blow the case wide open. And it will turn out that I'm right. The stories match. In one of Bianca's lesser-known published diaries, she mentions a "P." P wants to take a conflict to Judge Judy, or so Bianca claims in an entry. Speculations abound, but to my knowledge, nobody's suspected Pam. Yet the few times I've ventured into her yard, I could hear the infamous vocal fry from Pam's den before I even stepped onto her porch. A show application was once placed in my mail stack by mistake since we're right beside each other.

All this covert sneaking around is really paying off. Skin that's removed is called a hide, so maybe mine's just been practicing. It's been preparing for some abstract, future success.

9

THE GARLIC BREAD STAYS HERE

MY EMPLOYERS ARE impressed by the Pam theory. It checks out. They say I'm ready for "the next level," whatever that means. The big leagues. I'm not trying to ruin a nice moment, but I think I'd rather they put me in my place. Maybe I'll take cover until this whole thing blows over. I still don't know who I'm dealing with.

Out past the high-tension power lines and skunk cabbage, where both the deer and the teenagers take to drinking and dating, Bianca and her assistant Trish walk beside the manmade lake. Perched atop our town, you can see the zoos of residential zones unfurling from there.

Trish is very…kempt. She wears heavy pleats.

I circle them but it's really closer to a rhombus. I rhombus them. Awaiting the day when Bianca and I can be within shouting distance from each other in the physical and emotional sense.

Before I can detect the best eavesdropping location, Bianca waves me over. She looks calm, probably because she's completely unattached to any covert assignments or murky discrepancies.

"Tina, is it?" Bianca asks me.

"Tori, actually."

"We wanted to get your read on something. I'm not trying to sound arrogant, you understand. It's just that I think—we think—someone is stalking me."

Inwardly, I diagram routes to the closest witness protection program.

"Oh, really? Huh. Well, maybe this person's just trying to get to know you. Come on, haven't you ever wanted to be a sightseer in someone else's life?"

If you can't tell by now, my responses are pretty much always exclusively based on whether or not I can see a situation coming.

"If I've learned anything from humanity, it's that you need to keep your wits where I can see them. About you. I mean, keep your wits about you. It could be like having a stray cat."

I guess stalking doesn't work the same way as pet ownership. They've let me continue with this panicked conjecture for far too long.

Trish and Bianca look at each other.

"I'll take that into consideration," Bianca finally says.

"And do you have any clue who this supposed stalker might be?" I ask, acting casual. Totally *caszjh*.

Get to the part where you mine my soul for shame, I think. Get to the part where I'm doomed. I could work at a shipyard. Measuring the circumference of commercial lobsters might invigorate me. That abundant, seaworthy lifestyle is calling. Someday Bianca will be comforted by the proof that someone— really, multiple someones—cared about her so much.

"Trish has a list of, um, suspects I guess," Bianca says.

"So, what does your husband think about all this?"

Those words gargle up from my esophagus. The last time I saw Ryan he was breaking into his own home.

"He's on a business trip," says Trish, even though I wasn't asking her.

That doesn't give me anything. His pursuits have probably been romantic enough to skate by. We all know he harbors feelings for his wife's stalker underneath everything else.

"He's actually in Bianca's hometown right now. Can you guess where she's from?" Trish asks me.

"The Disney vault?"

They laugh and start walking again on cue, like dried up synchronized swimmers.

"Let me know how it goes!" I shout.

They pretend not to hear me and discuss some beef between the neighborhood watch and the historic preservation society.

I pass an old lady on the way back to my house. She's rocking on her front porch wearing a neon construction vest. I guess you can never be too careful. From an attraction standpoint, her bird feeder is missing the birds entirely. They're chirping away in a nearby tree.

Our landlord's in the yard when I get back. I ask him how he's doing as he evaluates our siding.

"Things are pretty good. You could say I have a new lease on life," he says, laughing enough for the both of us.

"I bet you say that to all your tenants."

"Quiet. Your voice is carrying," he says, looking around.

"Carrying what?"

I stare into his meringue hair and wait for the mysteries of life to reveal themselves to me.

"Here's some unsolicited advice, hon. Hold your liquor like you hold a grudge," he says while rummaging around in his van with the door open.

He extracts two thick slabs of garlic bread, holding one in each hand.

I guess I'm looking at them for too long because then he says, "These are both for me."

I wait for him to leave. He lives on the other side of town, across the street from an old train station with its immovable train lost to time and human intervention in the form of paint coats and city planning.

He finishes up whatever he's doing and packs up his van.

I flag him down as he backs out of the driveway.

"The garlic bread stays here," I say into his cracked window. "Nice try."

I disappear into our house. It's understood that our landlord gets too involved. He intrudes. There goes the solitude but here comes the decent rent.

After a full day of reconnaissance, I typically sweep our floors under cover of night. I open all the windows to air out the house from Allison's experiments in fermentation and find the broom. I reflect on the fact that taking things at face value really depends on the face in question. And wonder what else can be filtered through these window screens besides homemade kimchi.

10

SHOCK VALUE

THE DEATH THREATS continue. Allison doesn't appear too concerned. So how bad could they be? Unless they're only directed at me and she wants this place all to herself. I ignore them, same as always.

Since my run-in with Bianca, she's installed a mannequin in her front room, aligned with the large picture window for all to see, at Trish's prompting. Trish crouches beside it throughout the day to alter its position.

If only I were a real stalker. They wouldn't know what to do with me. Still, how much do they know? I'll let them leer at me as much as they want. Let's continue this charade.

Everybody's allowed exactly one delusion each. That's how it goes. It's only fair. To keep going in life. Any more than that and you're getting greedy. This is how the world works. I'm just pleased she's finally taken an interest in me.

Something Bianca probably doesn't suspect: I've constructed a replica of our neighborhood in a corner of the secret passageway. All the major landmarks are represented.

My sleuthing skills can take me about as far as my work in miniatures. Which is to say I wouldn't cut it in either market for very long. Where could a gal like me find someone to marvel at her tiny hot tub or equally tiny sinkhole covered by a—yes, a tiny gazebo.

Allison's twin is visiting. Her name is Mallison. I am serious. They've fused themselves to the passageway's walls, perhaps admiring my methods. They're here to lather on the admiration it seems.

"You're supposed to do something about this now," Allison says.

Apparently, I need to settle a dispute. Clear one of their names over some ordeal not even worth mentioning.

"Pick a side," Mallison chimes in.

How should I break it to them that my side-picking days are over? This isn't the time nor the place to act like a concerned citizen. You'd think they'd tone down the pageantry amid such a resplendent display. But they don't. And they never will.

I close my eyes, spin around a few times with my pointer finger extended, and stop whenever it feels right. Mallison prevails. They earnestly accept my verdict.

I rush past them to make a gig. We're opening for a band called Food Pyramid Scheme, a personal favorite. Well, we aren't so much opening for them as playing the open mic portion before them.

Our bass player Reggie found a free car under the overpass. The only problem is it's a limo. I agree to a ride from him just to see how it feels.

Everybody can smell me. I reek of piquant nervous sweats and compensatory perfume.

Vic has the best seat in the house: right beside me and an empty cooler.

The room's pretty empty when we arrive. Fortunately for this bar, I've never met a crowd I couldn't work. Food Pyramid Scheme is secondary. These attendees are all waiting, begging to be led astray. They can't get enough of our exuberance. Reggie walks onto the stage, already shirtless before we've begun. He leaves out any pectoral guesswork on the audience's part.

To warm them up, Reggie hand draws each one of their moms.

Meanwhile Vic tends to my accidental hot sauce goatee.

"Just leave it," I say. "It fits the mood."

One of the bartenders gestures to me like he wants us to stall some more. I ask Reggie if he can draw their fathers too.

"Not this group," he shudders.

He goes backstage to make personal calls instead.

I eavesdrop while the rest of our band tends to our new fans, but all I hear from Reggie's conversation is, "Not in my condition," and "There's no coming back from that."

At the end of the night, Vic tells me what happened to Bruce at the border. They used to play poker together. He heard from their mutual cronies that officials detained him for having the same name and constellation of face moles as someone who was not allowed to enter Canada. Vic's sources say he should be back home by now.

Naturally, I scope out his house the following morning. The

developing scene at Bruce's house feels off because it is. They were all a bunch of lies. Or at least the returning home part.

A dogwood blooms in his front yard, accentuating the hide-a-key rock beneath it.

For whatever reason, his couch pillows are arranged in the shape of a heart. If you meet someone who arranges anything in the shape of a heart, you run. Don't ask any questions.

I'm not sure why I decided to break and enter. I'd like to think it was to find a clue, for Bruce's sake. The townspeople have all hung up their skates since his roller disco has been out of commish. And don't get me started on the addicts at his racetrack.

I rummage through his cupboards. He's the only person I've ever met without a junk drawer. There's not even a rubber band or a paperclip in here.

The bathroom door is askew. I see a bejeweled arm in the mirror. Bianca is here.

"Don't make this a big production," she says, slinking out into the kitchen.

Bianca is here.

"Did Trish send you?" she asks.

"No," I manage to say.

"I know where all this is going," she starts.

Bianca is here.

I can only stare.

"Can I speak freely or what?" she asks.

"Go on."

Point is she may know where all this is going, but I've got nothing.

"There are just a few pictures and assorted memorabilia I need to pick up. You see, I have reason to believe Bruce isn't coming back."

She feels so caught that she doesn't even ask what I'm doing here.

"You want to see for yourself? You might never get this chance again."

She says this like she's more famous than she is. Like she can see her future laid out in front of her.

We traipse upstairs. She opens a cigar box that's filled with human teeth, a Swiss Army knife, a stack of photographs, some baseball cards, and indecipherable foreign coins. She flips through the photograph stack and stops.

"Here's when he ate a live frog in front of everyone. Said he could feel it ribbiting for hours inside of him."

It'd be better if I knew who "everyone" was, but I don't push my luck.

There's one thing that doesn't add up: No Bs appear in her published diary entries. However, I've seen what I needed to see. I will go quietly.

11

WHERE YOU LOST ME

I WAIT FOR Allison to stop crying. She makes herself known in my bedroom doorway. She's also somehow eating a bagel between sniffles.

Annoyed at her hovering, I ask, "Which one of you is the evil twin?"

"She just told me after I cleaned up at Bruce's racetrack a couple years ago that I really let myself go. I let all the winnings get to my head. So, who do you think is the evil one?"

"Did she leave?"

Allison nods and says, "She also told me she thinks my marriage is falling apart."

"Wait, you're married?"

She tries to clear the air by changing the subject. "Hey, what do you think of bunk beds?"

She holds up a diagram. She's put a lot of thought into this. "You mean for you and Mallison? Or for us?"

"For us, of course. That way we can devote my old room to performances and spycraft."

Allison is famous for her house shows. She mostly stations

herself in a corner mewling and draping over the drapes, some sort of meta statement of which I'm unqualified to interpret. She usually casts me as the "forest floor," which gives me a chance to lie dormant while pacifying her at the same time. Still, I'm sick of putting on a show every time her friends come over.

I was supposed to be at a dentist appointment right now, but they're rehabbing the building. If I'm literally waiting for them to construct a waiting room, does that make it somehow more of a waiting room than it was before?

Allison inventories the amount of "everything bagel" seasoning on her bagel, then hurls it against our bathroom door. The bagel is never to be seen again.

12

DEAD GIVEAWAY

IN THE EVENT of a Hard Rock Cafe, situate yourself as close to the memorabilia as possible. This way, you can consult their beefy tees anytime you like, assured anew that whatever you're wearing, you are not wearing a Hard Rock Cafe beefy tee.

A guy named Salem is expecting me. He's in an all-strings quartet called Strung Out. We made an arrangement a long time ago to survey each other's musical careers for glaring errors. We meet in the perfect place to give up hope.

I got here early. I hate when I show up someplace really having to use the bathroom first thing, so I always arrive first whenever possible.

"Do you have any Margaritaville hoodies on hand?" a man at the table right beside me asks a waiter.

His comment smudges the atmosphere like a well-handled menu.

"I'll let Jimmy Buffet speak for himself," says the waiter, slamming down a receipt.

I move one table over as a buffer.

Salem enters the restaurant, gives me a hug, and says, "I think I would make a really good getaway driver."

Not much else happens. We mill about.

Driving back, our local "hits of yesterday and today" station starts playing Haddaway's "What is Love?" The driver in front of me bobs his head over and over in a spasm-like fashion, apparently attuned to the same wavelength.

Here I am scrambling back to the neighborhood to erase my tracks from the night before. You see, Bruce owns buried treasure, and Bianca knows where to look, but not the precise coordinates. I know that because I watched her dig up half his backyard in search of the loot by the glow of a security spotlight protruding from Bruce's overly paranoid next-door neighbor.

Trish had started drawing up plans for a moat around Bianca's house after getting exasperated with manning the front-window mannequin, but I think Bianca's since talked her down. I see her rotate the thing every now and then, probably questioning who the real imposter is while she's at it.

I still can't really tell if they consider me a suspect. Maybe I'm more of a tragic figure.

Bianca's getting another book deal out of this stalker scenario. She'll be rewarded for her fame with more fame. I think we can all agree you can't solve the public eye with more publicity.

An old TV is curbed out front across the street, printed in the general direction of Bruce's house and in all likelihood his treasure. Contrived entertainment is a farce compared to the bounty of one's mind. That neighbor's better off without it. Television might be a lie, but I'm lurking under true pretenses.

And although my employers seem to be actively ignoring me, I patiently await further instructions and gather what I can in the meantime.

Allison happens to be roaming the sidewalks. I pull over and roll down the passenger side window.

"Get in."

She complies, then keeps asking me questions about what constitutes a nervous breakdown. I refrain from taping her mouth shut as we aim for the driveway.

I take her inside and show her where I tilt my head toward the ceiling to scream intermittently as part of my self-administered scream therapy sessions. I do most of my screaming at home. As long as Pam doesn't make a big deal out of the noise pollution. I encourage Allison to give it her best shot. She lets out an exemplary yelp. Beginner's luck, I guess.

"From the top," I say. She continues.

"I've never understood human attachments," I coach, "but ceilings—ceilings don't ask anything of you."

We're all the sum of what we do or don't do with the stuff screams are made of, I tell her between bellows.

13

PACE YOURSELF

EVER SINCE I slighted Allison by refusing to bunk with her in actual bunk beds she's been slipping these especially formal notes in the crack of my bedroom door on expensive stationery. Maybe this is a way of distancing herself, though it seems to have the opposite effect.

Regardless, she displays remarkable penmanship. She's also been refusing to mop the floors.

Meanwhile, I've become so overtaken with the case that Bianca can no longer exist outside of my gaze. Like an elementary school teacher found shopping at a grocery store. Impossible.

And get a load of this: I've started receiving a lot more requests for freelance work and invitations to apply for real jobs. The kind of thing I've been actively avoiding (but secretly longing for) by taking this fake spy gig. A dubious amount of opportunities lie before me. Some of them are from folks in the neighborhood watch, even. So, they are either a) changing their minds about me b) trying to trick me c) impressed by how often I've been seen out with Bianca and want to be proved wrong.

In my many years of brushing shoulders with people and minding my own theatrics, demand for my professional skills has never been higher.

It goes without saying I rejected them all.

And here's Allison, opening her mouth while giving me a look, then closing it. Decidedly not speaking to me still. Decidedly not mopping either. It's up to me to both carry on verbalized conversations and slop soapy water around in this household, quite possibly for good.

This is how I end up sheepish and pliable in a throng of nearly nude neighbors.

Everyone's invited to this kid's birthday party. They've hired an unofficial petting zoo. The event gives them a chance to show off their pool too. Bare skin and dangerous reptiles don't really seem to mix well. I'm around to catch the indignities that result.

All the regular faces run rampant near the foodstuffs. There's nothing discreet about which vegetation is set aside for the animals, and which is set aside for the humans, and I wonder if it angers them. The caged ones, I mean.

There's an old lady who owns a house positioned way too close to an already treacherously winding and narrow road outside of our neighborhood with alligators, snakes, and the like dwelling in dimly lit tanks amid her basement and a few potbellied pigs out back. She smokes light cigarettes with packaging catered specifically to women. The family must've hired her to save a buck.

James, a guy who lives four houses down, circulates in geometric-patterned swim trunks, giving everyone a good view of the scar from his hunting accident. That's sportsmanship for you, I guess.

I lean on the temporary fencing. One of these pigs has the face of my dead grandmother. I try not to think about it. This one strays from the rest of the drove. Somewhere, years from now, she'll still be expressing a deep disappointment in me and it'll be written all over her little pig face.

James cracks open his third beer beside the snack table.

"Is there any reason why these two ketchup bottles should not be joined together in holy matrimony," he says to nobody.

"James," I intervene, "what I'm about to tell you might seem forward, but please, pace yourself."

I don't go into the grandmother pig, how guilt tripping her relatives probably pulls her from one moment to the next in a gesture that goes beyond whatever tumult took place in her sty. I file this withholding away as an integral personal accomplishment.

James tells me he used to be a mountaineer. He chronicles his various escapades in high altitudes, tampering with the box I've already placed him in.

The birthday kid opens some presents but keeps getting distracted by the alligator's allure. Can't say I blame him. He opens a gift bag that contains an illustrated book, one of many starring an orphan who runs away to a riverboat casino. Kids' books are always about orphans. Some propaganda about familial radicalization.

Then it happens like this: Cops pull up to the party house. This isn't a noise complaint though. This is about Bruce.

I talk to them willingly. I flip through photographs of new evidence because they make me flip through photographs of new evidence. They question me and several others.

They found Bruce's briefcase buried in the lot behind his roller disco. It's the kind with those little ridged dials that you want to sink your fingernails into. The cops' pictures are clear enough to see that the combination on it was set to all zeros. His initials are on there too. It says "GBL" nice and large on a gold plate.

I know what's coming.

I go with my instincts.

That would be just like me to solve this case while everyone's got Bugles dangling from their fingertips and chlorine slowly erasing all the color from their bright bathing suits. But this revelation's a little too clean. I must play back the tapes in a proverbial sense. That's what published diaries are for.

I escape on an empty pedal tavern abandoned in the cul-de-sac, which makes for a furiously slow getaway.

If I'm correct, I'll reward myself with a popsicle while tinkering with my town replica for the thrill of it. What else do you want from me?

PART II

14

VICTORY BUCKET

THERE'S ONLY ONE thing I can do. I have to pack my bags. I must feast on my own success. This is my turn now. There's a reputation to think about. Up until this point, I've been merely spectating. Sidelining. Waiting for someone to hand over the goods. To establish me. Rather than taking the reins and becoming the mystical musical outlaw I was made to be.

That sort of thing.

Let me back up.

I'm talking about Rhonda & the Sandwich Artists. We've been invited on tour. To be associated with this particular band would go a long way.

But I digress. When I arrived home from that kid's birthday party last night, I pushed the pedal tavern into the ravine and covered it with some loose leaves. Placing a handful of leaves over one of the seats I noticed a hard, speckled mound. On closer inspection, the mound was actually a turtle. I'm not sure if she escaped from the unofficial petting zoo or if she arrived straight from nature itself, but I don't care. She chose to hunker down in the pedal tavern and that's all that matters. I am overcome with admiration for her. I named her Erin before I'd even brought her inside.

I adopted her in a sense. Like you knew I would.

And overnight, this tour lands in our laps. A chance to regroup. Erin is heedless of my aspirations, barely blinking in the corner. I don't trust Allison caring for her while I'm gone. She'll have to tag along.

We'll lodge in Reggie's limo and shower at truck stops when we can. I'll acquire a little shower cap for Erin. Why not.

Speaking of Allison, she looks a little too relieved to have me off the premises. Plus her notes tell me the death threats have gotten "more specific."

I break the news to my employers, hedging my words and sounding as dolorous as I can muster. They reply immediately and rather coldly: *Sounds great. Let us know when you'd like to resume with the project. There's absolutely no rush.*

They say "no rush" repeatedly throughout the email. As if all my efforts are meaningless.

Once Reggie rounds the corner in his limo, I push the espionage project out of my mind.

I open the door. Everyone's already tucked into their seatbelts and digging into their car snacks before we've even reached the county line.

"What's this?" I ask Reggie, holding up a galvanized pail from the backseat and positioning it in the rearview mirror for him to peek at while he drives.

"Oh, that? That's my victory bucket."

"Uh," I say.

"The victory bucket stays. It's part of the deal," he says.

"Is this because I wanted to bring Erin?"

I caress her tank. I don't ask what a victory bucket is.

Vic clears his throat. He passes around a laminated list of roadside attractions for our scrutiny. There's a lot on here but I skim a few items:

- Paul Bunyan
- World's tallest thermometer
- House made out of beer cans
- Water tower in the shape of the largest catsup bottle in the world
- Preserved human brains in the basement of the Yale medical library

How about that.

"Is this tour a game to you? Well guess what. I already know all the games," says Laura.

I'm sorry, I don't think I've mentioned her yet. She's our drummer. She just needs less caretaking than the other two so she's easy to miss.

"From my studies, all of these attractions are open to the public," Vic says.

"Everybody's agendas are of little concern to me," she says.

Reggie starts tearing up. The full water works are out to play. Nice touch.

As I was telling you, I guess you could say our band has

made it. We are cloaked in power. We are too crafty for our own good. It's actually not helping, now that I think about it.

I notice that Vic's wearing a windbreaker embroidered with our band name on it—as if he's always worn it, like it's always been there.

At a rest area on the state line, Reggie pulls over to peruse the vending machines. Next thing I know, he's running into the woods behind a building labeled COMFORT STATION. He is forgoing and retreating in one fluid motion.

There he goes. He's hiding behind a tree draped in caution tape halfway up a hill. Except that everyone can see him, and everyone watched him do it.

Laura throws sticks at him until he complies. She knows these guys respond well to the tough love routine. She also knows that I do not.

Somehow, we make it to our first show.

A guy carries around what looks to be a child's brightly colored boombox from a couple decades ago. He presses play on a laugh track after telling a joke or insulting someone. This goes on for much longer than I think it will.

Every time.

All night.

"You won't catch me telling others how to feel about my jokes," says Reggie. And I believe him.

It's only natural that traveling would finally catch up to me. I just didn't expect it to be within 24 hours of our departure.

I could go back to school. I have numerous personality theories that are surprisingly complex. Like the subset of people who are a) grade school teachers b) have really bubbly handwriting—I'm talking eerily similar to everyone else in the group—and c) love Mexican food. There are also the folks who eat those single slices of grocery store cake sitting alone in their cars like they're trying to get away with something. This group struggles with buying way too many t-shirts.

I could work with these theories. There's more where these came from. I don't have to stay here if I don't want to.

"A sandwich for one of the sandwich artists," says an especially kind bartender, sliding a plate in front of me.

After a few bites I'm a whole new person. I'm ready to storm the stage.

15

A SERIES OF OVERCORRECTIONS

BY THE TIME we reach our next tour destination, I'm irreparably wounded. Colors I didn't think were naturally occurring begin to surface on my skin. Everyone else is intact. If you will.

Vic's experiment is getting out of hand. I won't stand for it. Laura could take or leave his makeshift laboratory.

He bought one of those science experiment kits at a giant truck stop.

"Shouldn't you be wearing safety goggles? Or gloves?" I ask.

"What are safety goggles?" he asks.

Laura pulls her phone out of her back pocket like a cop drawing a pistol.

"Should I call urgent care?"

I assure her that won't be necessary. There's no going back from this and that's fine. I think I've become all knowing. I am now aware of things that haven't been invented yet. I'm rendering my roommate's psychic services obsolete.

The vial lay in a cup holder, thick with possibilities. Transcending whatever the manufacturer originally intended for this product. Beckoning me to gain notoriety in yet another professional field.

The burning sensation on my arm, though menacing, feels a bit invigorating, I'll admit. Really those two words—menacing and invigorating—are interchangeable though, right? In all of life. Probably.

Anyway, I convince Vic to name his firstborn baby after me to make up for his major scientific failure.

And while we're on the subject of psychics, I might as well tell you that Allison keeps sending me those letters on her fancy stationery, only now that we're on the road, she's sending them through the United States Postal Service. I don't even know how she keeps track of where we are or what addresses she uses. Laura keeps handing them to me somehow. Allison writes that since I've left the death threats have stopped piling up. They've stopped completely. I add her letters to my files.

My fellow band members haven't said anything about Allison's letters and how weird it is that she writes so often, but I know they're thinking it.

Reggie keeps trying to initiate a food fight. He's working too hard. It all feels contrived. We shrug him off each time he mentions the idea.

Obviously, things are really heating up. Food fight? No food fight. Experiments? No more experiments. We go on like this for a while.

The headlining band, the whole reason we're sequestering ourselves in Reggie's limo, is right in front of us. They have a nice van. We all got walkie talkies for the trip even though we could just use our phones. Laura cashed in a few favors to get us here. Animal Vegetable Mineral is a pretty high-profile band, if I haven't made that clear yet. There are a lot of bands out there trying to sound like they're from the 80s. And Animal Vegetable Mineral is no different. But I go along with it. There isn't an objection objectionable enough to stop us.

I know I paused the case once we left. Still, I can't help but drive by Bianca's childhood home while we're out here. We're in the area. Sort of. Doesn't matter that I orchestrated it this way.

I doctored the tour dates to include an afternoon middle school assembly at her alma mater. So what. Nobody bothered to question me.

To seal the deal, I met Bianca's old middle school principal in an online chat room. Since then, I've been turning down his invitations left and right. I've trained Vic to tend to the principal's messages. Standard procedure. He slings polite rejections as instructed anywhere we can access wifi.

Bianca's old middle school looks like any other middle school. I'm wearing an outfit I bought after seeing her in it on the day she did that morning show interview. Full disclosure: I fancy myself a doppelgänger of hers. If not physically then maybe spiritually.

"This guy is rather taken with you," Vic says, closing his laptop.

Don't I know it.

"It appears he's fallen out of public favor since the knife fight," he continues.

Principals. The pinnacle of dominance.

I try to make myself scarce in the auditorium but we're on stage. We are discernible from the gathering of pubescents kicking the auditorium's pull-down chairs. They're unflappable. Unlike their chairs, which make a loud whomp-whomp-whomp every time they get up and down during our show.

We manage to perform under the harsh lights and harsher live-action display of morphing bodies below us.

Reggie insists we order from Arby's afterward.

A balding man behind the counter greets Reggie by name.

"How does he know you?"

"I've already been here five times today."

We collectively tilt our heads at him.

Laura pulls me back by my tainted arm.

"There's something you should know about Reggie. He's a part-time hitman. That's how he was able to afford his calf implants," she says.

I gather she's suggesting that he is more dangerous than I realized.

I crack my back and roll my neck instead of responding. I'm sore from all that riding in the limo we're doing. But really, my bad posture is just an apology for existing. I can't carry on with the charade any longer.

Reggie's plan is simple: Collect enough Arby's combos throughout multiple trips (so as not to appear too suspicious, as if that's somehow better than entering the place multiple times in one day) to host a successful food fight. Yes, he's still insisting on a food fight.

"You'll be so changed that you'll become more like yourself than you were before," Reggie says.

I look at Laura, then say, "That could be arranged."

"Really?"

The Arby's parking lot is obliterated beyond recognition. The meats? Well, we have them now. Or more like the pavement. Those parking block things—I call them concrete Kit Kats—are stained with innumerable sauces.

"You know, they say touring provides priceless memories, and forgive me for saying so, but I feel it applies here," Reggie says.

He wipes sesame seeds off his forehead.

To come down from his food fight high, Reggie squats in an abandoned house overnight without us. Some extroverted kids from the assembly told us it's haunted. I watch the front door for hours, but nobody goes in or out. I continue on foot down the block, thinking about what it'd be like to have a healthy relationship with sandwiches.

16

STALL TACTICS

WHAT REMAINS of the limo explodes through a dark cloud encircled in flames.

"What about my Selena poster? It was still in there," says Vic.

He'd tacked a poster of the murdered mononymous singer on the limo's ceiling two days ago.

"What about the rest of our stuff," says Laura.

Too late.

None of us goes to the trouble of calling the authorities.

"I found that limo under the overpass fair and square," Reggie says, spitting on the ground.

Chrrrsh.

"Attention! Attention! Animal Vegetable Mineral, can you hear me?" I say through a walkie talkie.

Chrrrsh.

"AVM, are you there? Over."

Chrrrsh.

I'm just glad Harvey from AVM didn't have to see this. He's the most talented member of the band. He brandishes a woodblock on stage for special occasions. His beloved woodblock would've been the first to go.

"They're probably asleep. Like we should be," says Vic.

"There was a blown fuse. You can't convince me otherwise," says Laura.

And since she's the only one who's ever been a mechanic, we all stay quiet.

Before the limo was completely engulfed, we were able to grab a smattering of essentials, like the walkie talkies and Erin the turtle. I found a crumpled note underneath a seatbelt clasp. I save it for later when nobody's looking.

Erin seems a little dazed and maybe annoyed but otherwise healthy. I'm not really sure what a healthy turtle is supposed to look like though.

"Maybe this is good. A rejuvenating event in our lives. There's no evidence of pilfering someone else's vehicle now. This expunges us from the record," I propose, attempting to smooth things over.

Insects of all types start to swarm us. It's an ambush. They're toying with us while we're at our most vulnerable.

"Bugs don't bother me. They know I bite back," Reggie says.

We don't respond. We each have our separate reasons.

A gnat flies out of my ear that I didn't know was there.

What else happens?

We get Animal Vegetable Mineral on the line. They agree to let us ride with them on a temporary basis. There's not much room in their van apparently, no matter how luxe it appears from the outside. Plus the sheer fact that a vehicle exploded on our watch implicates us. They force us to sign an agreement in triplicate.

Before our gig the following day, Vic pauses at the entrance. Everyone knows he's deeply afraid of revolving doors, both in their literal and metaphorical forms. And here they are, with no regular doors on either side like you typically see.

Vic slinks through the back alley in disgrace.

While we're setting up, a stranger at the corner table offers to pay for one of my kidneys. He'll even extract it for me.

"How's that strike you?"

"What's the black-market rate for a kidney these days?" I ask. "I'd like to see some figures first."

There's nothing wrong with knowing all your options.

He promises to administer a local anesthetic at the appointed time. I can even pick which kidney I want to give up. He completely ignores my question. Strike one.

I can't help but suspect he's done this before. His orderly matter suggests a pattern. Perhaps he comes from a long line of public organ extraction and sales. He probably learned how to operate under the tutelage of his own father, or grandfather even. Everybody wants to retire eventually.

I wonder how he picked me. Or if he asks people indiscriminately. What is the criteria here? Can he tell that my kidneys are particularly alluring?

"Crunch those numbers for me. Then, and only then, will I consider your arrangement," I say as a bartender drops a plate in front of him.

"This is a kidney-free environment," the bartender says.

I make eyes at the cheeseburger in between us. The bartender walks away.

I disengage from the conversation, but not before taking a fry from the stranger's plate.

I'll admit to wanting more of his secret black-market thoughts. I should've asked follow-up questions before making a final stand and rendering myself inoperable. But there's no getting around the possibility that he's trying to frame me. Nobody will tarnish my career but me. That's something even Reggie can understand.

Our band is gaining traction with this audience. We're wrapping up, but they want an encore. We've run out of songs right when we've established ourselves.

"Leave them wanting more. It's time for my signature move," Reggie says.

Here goes.

He pushed us into the van and gets in the driver seat.

"The victory bucket is now a part of me," he says.

We're waiting to find out what that means just like everybody else. We're all dying to get to the bottom of this bucket, which seems like a relatively easy thing to do given how shallow it is. The bucket in question is widely believed to be a red herring, but nobody has figured out what the red herring would be needed for.

Reggie parks us at a racetrack. He keeps muttering "my signature move" to himself. He practically sprints into what look to be horse stables, bucket in tow.

"Somebody should follow him for some kind of…proof," Laura says.

I volunteer. If you volunteer for things long enough with this crowd you can erase some of your more unforgivable acts.

I peek into the stables right when he's turning off a spigot. He carries the now-full bucket of water over to the horses, placing it in front of each pen one at a time. He gauges their reactions, recording them in a notebook he's pulled from his back pocket.

Once he's covered all the horses, he dumps out any trace of water and leaves.

Despite the duffel bag full of cash, he ultimately wins once he's had a chance to bet on those horses, his victory bucket method fails to catch on, both with us and in society at large. A formula like that can't lead to anything good. We all have our limits. We renounce the victory bucket before we've begun.

Back in the van, Laura pulls up a video on her phone. It's a news clip. There's Vic. He's supposedly made the rotation at every major news hour. His face has never looked so distinguished. They labeled him as a "bystander" underneath a fake name he must've given them, and I think they could've dug deeper there with his title. Otherwise, he couldn't ask for more from this coverage. He'd even plugged our show, but they cut him off mid-sentence.

From above, in what I can only assume is drone footage, you can see the rest of us hiding behind a semi and peering out sporadically to survey the scene. The limo flames on, burning bright into the night.

17

WHERE YOU LOST ME

YOU ALWAYS WANT to avoid lying to hotel clerks. But here I am lying to a hotel clerk. The rest of the band made me do it. I give them all what they want to see. I'm volunteering again whether I like it or not. Of course I volunteered. I invented volunteering.

The hotel clerk just asked me whether we're here for the Possum Festival. I say yes. Definitely. How could we miss it?

"Not if Big Scott has anything to say about it," he says, and begins to laugh an unearthly laugh. He mangles my ears with his volume. I'll need to see a specialist before we reach our next stop.

In the aftermath, I register what he's said. Big Scott. I wonder what this means. What could befall me if I conduct a mission to infiltrate the Possum Festival? The full possum treatment. I'm not trying to sound ambitious or anything, but someday I'd like to star in a movie "as herself." Big Scott seems like the guy to get me there. I have no idea if this is true.

My fellow band members wanted me to lie about the reason we're here, but they weren't specific about the details.

They wanted to avoid any stereotypes that might arise if staff heard rock stars were in the building.

"I'll never forget you," I say to the clerk, turning away with a mini paper folder full of room keys.

Animal Vegetable Mineral always stays in hotels when they tour. They also have a manager. Maybe a publicist too. Your personhood is amplified once you garner something of a following. Or so it appears from the outside.

Reggie seconded their decision. Back in their van, he'd said, "I mean how can we sleep in a place like this?"

He slid around on a seat in an exaggerated fashion like an actor from an infomercial attempting pretty much anything. His arms swung in ever-widening circles like he was falling while in a reclined position.

"This is basically the same sleeping setup as the limo," Laura countered.

Reggie offered to pay for our sleeping arrangements with his duffel bag full of cash at first, then remembered he needed to pay somebody off.

I hand Laura the folder of room keys.

She validates my interaction with the clerk by saying, "Don't let it get to your head."

Then she gives me a look like she always does.

"Doesn't seem like you tried very hard to get that AAA discount though."

Vic and Reggie are lulled by an overburdened freezer in the alcove with all the marked-up refreshments and supplies.

A tubular frozen treat signals to them beneath the glass

doors. It appears to glow from the inside, and I realize that lights are probably installed in there.

We take a room on the fourth floor at the end of a hallway with a window overlooking the hotel parking lot and some massive signs leading to prevalent fast food chains.

There's no need for us to grab our belongings. Animal Vegetable Mineral rolls past us with those carpeted carts.

I roam the hallway until I reach a stairwell. I pull out the crumpled paper I retrieved from the limo before it completely exploded.

The paper is another letter from Allison. She must've run out of her stationery. I skim past all the boring parts until I get to an unavoidable statement. She says there's an update on Bruce. He's been declared dead. I think maybe they could be wrong about his death. He's probably quite skilled at hiding from the police. But Allison goes on to write that they've recovered his body. Usually, they're rather thorough with bodies.

I make my way back to our room. Yes, we're all sleeping in the same room. I broach the subject with Laura, debriefing her on the recent developments. She says she's never seen the letter before. She had no clue what'd happened to Bruce. She recrumples the paper and throws it in the garbage, no questions asked. Between you and me, regardless of how easily duped I often am, I believe her. No doubt people are plotting in this room, but nowhere so much as atop the air conditioning unit, where Vic and Reggie take turns with a pair of binoculars.

"You can see the venue from here," Vic says.

Reggie swings around, noticing me for the first time. "I've been expecting you," he says for no reason.

I gauge everyone's interest on the Possum Festival, thinking I can take them aside one by one to interrogate them about the crumpled note. Somebody please give me something I can use. But they choose to idle by the air vents. Recuperating! They call it recuperating!

"There's nothing out there for me," Reggie says.

He jumps on one of the king-sized beds with renewed vigor.

We cannot bring ourselves to leave the room until showtime. Why should I assume otherwise? Recuperating is no picnic, let me tell you.

I plot a way to trespass into the festival on my own, but even I'm not immune to the malaise that pervades our shared space.

"Who wants the vanity kit?" I ask from the bathroom.

They all step closer to me.

18

OVERBOARD

"WHAT DO YOU make of him?" Reggie asks me.

"I don't know. Something's not right. People still believe in topiary?" I say.

A shadowy profession, if you ask me. Which he did.

"Of course, if you attempt this, the whole topiary community might fold in on itself," I add.

He ignores me and says, "How well versed are you in maritime law?"

Things are getting away from us. He wants to stage a fake kidnapping. He thinks if he's able to pull this off he can avoid paying whoever he needs to pay and we can keep the duffel bag full of cash for touring expenses.

"I'm sorry, but I cannot take kidnapping lightly. Nor meddling with maritime law."

I'm not here to mop up his humiliation when everything goes south, that's for sure.

The guy he owes money to is a notable topiarist. And a pool shark.

"I knew a topiarist once," Vic chimes in.

It's clear Reggie has no discernible plan in mind.

What will become of me? What will become of my turtle? These thoughts press into my mind.

"If you see hedge trimmers in my hand, you'll know what to do," Reggie says.

I should've seen this coming as soon as he unzipped his bag of winnings. The bag I always imagined for him.

"Why can't you take your trusty victory bucket and go find the nearest racetrack? Earn some more cash and pay the guy off. Keep going until you want to stop. Isn't that how this is supposed to happen?" Laura says.

Reggie stares at her for multiple seconds. He gets up and walks out the door.

If his trick keeps working, I could put the Bianca investigation and this band behind me and devote my life to gambling. The way it should be.

Nah, that would be terrible.

19

WE'LL NEVER SPEAK
OF THIS AGAIN

I WILL BE back home in a week's time. On the day of Bruce's memorial service, actually. For the moment I am lost to the road.

But the worst part is probably over by now, right?

Reggie lifts the protective sheet he'd placed over the victory bucket. He takes the sheet out behind Animal Vegetable Mineral's van and torches it. He feels he has failed, which is probably true.

His failure is a message of some kind.

Reggie has been experimenting with the bucket at various racetracks across the country as time has allowed. The thing worked for every race. His methods were exquisite. And fairly discreet. The track owners were always caught unawares. Reggie naturally built no small amount of acclaim in certain betting circles. Gamblers wanted to associate with him all of a sudden. The effects were noticeable. He paid for everything.

Then, the last race left something to be desired. His chosen horse didn't even place. He's been forensically deconstructing the now-cursed metal pail ever since, trying to figure out how it changed into an ordinary one seemingly overnight.

We all have our limitations, and I guess objects are no different.

Reggie insists his bucket was compromised. He distributes revenge on an unknown aggressor in his dreams. We can hear him yelping at all hours of the night. He's rigged the van's trunk to be a hideout of sorts. So he can take calls in there and enact a somnambulant justice whenever he sees fit.

Laura says they have it on record that Reggie's dad never once smiled in his life and that his mother was a killing machine in the military. All of which must result in him carrying more than his fair share of emotional freight.

But what do I know.

I'm still keeping tabs on Bianca while I'm off the clock, don't you worry. Myths have started to collect around her. The stalker concept has morphed into a coup. There is purportedly a whole gang of lurkers after her now. And so basement dwellers along with live action role players—which is really more of a Venn diagram situation now that I think about it—are brandishing swords and guarding her driveway in the hopes of saving her life somehow. She is transmitting an aura of pure victimhood, and everyone is lapping it up. Maybe it's for the best that I'm not there to see it go down. Did I start the whole scandal in the first place? Does she know the stalker is in all likelihood me, but really, I'm just doing my job? Is she messing with me? Best to lay low. Even if laying low looks like jumping on numerous spotlit stages. Which in my case, it very much does. A special case.

But the worst part is probably over by now, right? As we've already established.

Vic asks me to go out for coffee with him. I wouldn't go so far as to say Vic is the kind of guy who talks loudly in public settings so that bystanders will overhear him. But his volume seems purposeful. We'll stick with that.

Vic and I find a table near the front windows of a place highly rated on an app that handles stuff like that. So we can be both seen and heard.

"As it happens you look good," Vic says.

I choose to hear it as a compliment.

"Thanks?"

"Let's get right to it," he says, then pauses to shake his head. "Nah, I dunno. I'm not even supposed to be talking to you."

"Huh?"

He sighs deeply to show hesitation, but he's not winning any awards with his acting.

"It's Laura. She's the one who's been sending you all those death threats in the mail."

"What are you talking about? How do you know about those?"

"She thought threatening you would be motivation for you. That you'd write better lyrics. You'd have more artistic sensibilities after going through a traumatic hardship."

I doubt it. I'll make inquiries though. I save the fact for later. I haven't ruled anything out.

Without meaning to, I laugh. I continue to laugh. It's getting painful.

"Keep it together. Contain yourself," Vic says, grabbing my hand.

But the worst part is probably over by now, right? And all of that.

"She knows what she's doing. You've improved."

"Is that why these threats have stopped since we left for the tour?" I manage to ask.

"Yeah. I thought you might've pieced things together at this point. Didn't mean to shock you."

Vic didn't have to divulge his findings. He's earned my trust. I have no choice but to tell him about the Bianca operation. That's what all the murderers say on those true crime shows: I had no choice.

To think I could've dealt with Laura mere moments ago. Right then and there in the van.

If her plan really worked, if I have improved, should I care?

I tell Vic about my investigation in great detail. I leave nothing out. Even the disguises I've incorporated. I have my reasons.

Eventually, he tells me that I can be dismissed. Either he's processing a lot of information at once or we'll never speak of this again.

Upon our return, I'm on the verge of proposing an emergency band meeting.

"You can come out now," I say to Reggie, knocking at the doors of the van's trunk.

He's communing with his bucket. Laura pretends not to see. Who even knows what goes on in there. Or what Animal Vegetable Mineral thinks of us after our displays.

Reggie asks permission to go to the bathroom.

Whatever new respect I've gained for him since this tour began froths over, falling several rungs in the process.

To improve the atmosphere, Vic sings Reggie a song with lyrics only they can understand.

The bucket in question is removed. That's the main thing.

Who will take me in once everything comes to light?

PART III

20

CUT TO THE CHASE

WE'RE PULLING UP into my driveway at long last. I start gathering my things. Erin the turtle looks relieved.

Vic is crossing off his giant list filled with points of interest. We'd made a good dent in it.

"The teapot," he mutters.

"What?" Laura says.

"I forgot about the world's largest teapot. I can't believe it."

"You missed more than that. There'll be another chance," she says.

"Gas up this van. We might as well start our second trip," Reggie shouts. I exit the vehicle while I still can.

The point is, a tour goes everywhere and nowhere at once. A band touring is really an exercise in courting danger.

I bet you want me to cut to the chase about what happened to Bruce. Yeah, well, so do I. Cops are still filing paperwork, but his death is a dead end in more than one sense of the term. Officially, natural causes. He simply died in his sleep. He was perfectly healthy. These things happen all the time, so they say.

Reggie insists on spreading a rumor that he was attacked by Bigfoot anyway.

They've even ruled out murder.

Reggie says you can never truly rule out murder.

As you can see, it's impossible for people to quit making up their own narratives, taking liberties and trading legends wherever they go.

I wave to the van as it creeps back down the road in reverse. We'll see each other almost too soon at something approximating a memorial service.

I heave my tortured luggage inside. Allison looms in the living room.

"Anything new?" I ask.

She shrugs. "They changed the school mascot. They're the space cadets now."

21

SHOWBOATIN'

I'M MAKING A wrong turn down a dim hallway. I'm not supposed to go any farther. There's a sign that reads EMPLOYEES ONLY.

People the world over have prevailed upon the funeral home's lackluster chapel. Bruce had powerful contacts. And here they are, cloaked in pretensions. Showboatin' around. Nobody likes a showboat.

Don't ask me how many folks have been lured here. Numbers never stay with me. Sometimes they don't even materialize to begin with.

The procession of neighborhood watchers drives me to a forgotten corridor with lopsided bookshelves. I banish myself until the most presentable guests have passed.

Looks like the whole neighborhood watch is in attendance. Liz seems to have given them some kind of dress code too. Snazzy black with a respectful splash of color.

They showboat around at length.

Allison and Popcorn sit in a loveseat by the double doors. A loveseat of all things. No coincidence in their selection of furniture there. I'm sure that's what's been going on while I've been away.

Allison catches me staring. She drags an imaginary zipper across her lips. Popcorn mouths "don't cross her" while wearing a fearful expression.

They're teeming with fresh romance, aren't they?

Pam finds my hiding place after about ten minutes of loitering.

"Are you alright?" she asks.

"I was shocked," I say.

"His passing is certainly unsettling to us all."

"No, I mean, I was shocked fiddling with that lamp over there. It wasn't plugged in. Gave me a bit of a jolt. It's too dark in here."

Pam takes the hint and scouts the area for a more sociable location.

Right when I think the service is set to begin, a funeral home employee comes out of the chapel and runs down the hall in question.

Anything could be down there.

I'm feasting on all the gossip from here without having to interact with anyone. For starters, a young woman walks in. She's a total stranger, but she also seems familiar.

Through the usual channels I learn that Bruce has a daughter. Her name is Memory.

That's her, right there.

Bruce's daughter is a great surprise to everyone, despite our predilection for spreading vaporous verbal delicacies. The block busybodies each have different answers. One says Memory lives in a group home for youths with mental disturbances. Another says she owns a boutique clothing label in the southwestern corner of Milan and that a large corporation modeled an iconic doll after her likeness.

Pam's husband Jeff shakes hands with her. He will refuse to wash said hand for the rest of the day.

I claim a seat in the chapel.

Up front, Bruce lies prone amid billowy satin. A samurai sword is tucked across his chest, supposedly purchased on the black market. Bruce is there, taking it all in. For eternity. His mortality appears malleable. That much I know.

Despite the cakey makeup, his face says: I see right through your game. He establishes dominance even in death.

Bianca is lined up in the first row as if she's the widow, in all likelihood gathering material for her new book. Ryan isn't beside her, but you already know who is. I can almost see the metal gear gleaming on Trish's backside. The one Bianca must have to wind up every morning to get her humming along.

The service begins. Attendees approach the podium one at a time to make vague declarations about Bruce's life on Earth. Nothing they say pertains to the investigation. They're too cautious of both giving something away and speaking ill of the deceased.

Is it my imagination or does Bianca keep looking back at Memory? Over and over, she turns her head. Then again, seated so close to the front, pretty much everyone is behind her.

Word of dinner afterwards filters through the rows of mourners, and I have to stop myself several times from calling it an "afterparty." Though that feels fitting for Bruce.

They settle on a restaurant where there's enough time, money, and absurdity to sculpt butter into alternate shapes, like roses and seashells. But I guess absurdity is born out of time and money, so there you go.

I find a new threat crumpled in my bag on the way out. At least I know who to blame.

Laura's "d"s look like little fists ready to punch me.

Memory declines an invitation to dinner, which isn't done in our neighborhood. The difference between her and me is that she gets away with it.

Let's see. Now that I'm back, I can continue cracking the case wide open. It just so happens I know where to look for the next big break. I'll pick up where I left off. But I need to get through dinner first. Admittedly, I pine for that intricately shaped butter.

22

FILL IN THE BLANK

I ENTER THE restaurant and find the table full of mourners. I make it in time to hear a standalone punchline.

"And the patient says, 'Tongue depressors aren't the only thing that's depressed today,'" some guy says.

"Oh, I hate it when that happens. Only hearing the end of a joke. Want me to tell it?" Pam asks me, scooting her chair over to make room.

"I'll take the end of the joke as long as I'm not the butt of a joke," Pam's husband says.

I wish I could've missed that joke instead.

Reggie's on my other side. He passes me a sleeve of saltines under the table. They're always with him. They're part of his regimen.

One falls to the floor between us.

Reggie introduces me to Shania, a cousin of Bruce's. She's a cheesemonger who arrived by boat yesterday morning.

The abandoned saltine is still at large under our feet. This saltine is indifferent to Shania the cheesemonger's presence.

It doesn't care about any of us. Eventually it gets tangled, torn asunder, crushed underfoot, and then encrusted into the patterned carpet.

Our server keeps calling the chocolate cake "transcendent." We must try the cake. It's transcendent.

Reggie orders the cake after she mentions it a third time while she's clearing our dinner plates.

The cake materializes before him. He dislodges a piece, holding it aloft on his fork tines.

"See you on the other side."

Liz patrols the table at an alarming rate, making what sound like incantations whose meanings are ungraspable.

Consulting with Pam, I decipher that she's talking about our community's plan to build a monument at the man-made lake. They'll be constructing a statue of Bianca with a placard and everything, which seems inappropriate given the fact that she's still alive and Bruce is freshly dead.

Not long after the unveiling ceremony, Allison will place a curse on the statue. It will forever be covered in bird droppings, food wrappers, and pollen. The real Bianca will remain untouched. This won't translate to a monumental voodoo doll, in other words.

On the way out, I look back. Allison is covering her eyes with the heels of her palms, knee deep in the bushes near the entrance, hoping to be seen. You can picture something else if you want. I've seen this before. There's a bus boy smoking beside her. He gets involved.

A handful of the funeral crowd is headed over to rummage

through Bruce's underground bunker for treasure. Or help clean it out. Same thing if you ask me.

That's enough exchanging pleasantries for me. Those people are no longer recognizable as fellow human beings. My limit is about four hours of socialization, tops.

I can't prove it, but I think Allison was being honest with me about her marital status.

I've gathered that Popcorn is her actual spouse. They were seated at the far end of our long dinner table. Every now and then, I could catch pieces of their conversation drifting down like an afterthought.

Popcorn suggested she close her psychic practice in favor of creating her own brand of kitchen appliances and cleaners called Counter Intuitive. She could actually use her chemistry degree. Later on, Allison mentioned that his bare feet brushing the hardwood always sounds less like a regular shuffle and more like a tsk-tsk-tsk. I guess they've somehow managed to establish a sort of truce by staying married and living in separate dwellings.

Cut to my house. Erin made an escape attempt while I was gone. Her head protrudes from her shell and lowers in disgrace. I worry there might be another uprising.

"How we interpret the silence of others reveals a lot about our past," I whisper to the turtle.

Everyone has that feeling of estrangement from their family, the notion that they might have been switched at birth. But I actually was. And it's such a played-out plot that nobody believes me.

My phone rings.

"I need to take this," I say to Erin.

I don't need to take this. I fabricate a sense of urgency so I can exit the room. I'm still mad at her about trying to leave the house. This is only a spam call. I breezily press decline once I'm on the stairs and out of view.

Footage of Bianca's appearance on the public access station calls to me from my computer. I play it back, categorizing her comments along the way. This footage has already given over all its secrets to me. All the secrets it could produce. Which isn't much.

The truth is I haven't put a ton of thought into my final presentation to my anonymous employers. I haven't done the homework because I've been busy living out my destiny as a rock star.

I fumble through my closet and extract our half of the walkie talkie set. Animal Vegetable Mineral never confiscated it. I switch it on and listen for them. I wait for them to tell me my fortune or give me advice or boost my confidence. I can't get through to them. They're not in range.

I can still taste the chocolate cake from earlier. Reggie let me have a couple bites. It wallows on my papillae, transcending time and space, life and death, cursed statues and seafaring cheesemongers.

23

AT YOUR DISPOSAL

WHEN YOU AREN'T paying attention, you end up at the edge of someone's property line, spying.

Bianca and Trish are each holding dusty roller skates dredged up from Bruce's underground bunker. I know because I am here watching them behind a row of shrubs. I'm a backyard stowaway.

Who knows what they did with the others. The post-funeral pilferers. Seems like everybody took a piece of the bunker as a memento and why wouldn't they. Here we call mementos "collector's items." Rumors have been harvested that Pam's husband emerged from the bunker with a taxidermied human hand. Which, if true, would be very much an illegal practice.

I've suspected all along that Bruce faked his own death to get the cops off his back. But there's no way he'd let Pam's husband of all people abscond with a human hand that's as preserved as his canned goods.

I remain at my station long enough to absorb the goings-on. I've recalibrated to solely perform undercover scenarios so that I can thwart any dealings with Trish. She's been acting like she doesn't know me. She hasn't come out and said it yet, but it's like I'm not supposed to address her directly. As if she's already in on it. My whole deal.

I cooperate. Even backyard stowaways have their rules.

I tamper with everyone's backyards on the way home, going to town on each manicured patch of grass in a vigorous fashion. Evoking the rage is all the rage. Or so I hear. I take my time unspooling the landscaping. You can imagine my surprise when nobody budges from their cozy interiors to unload on me.

Erin the turtle is encaged beside Allison in the living room when I return. Allison keeps consorting with Erin behind my back, like she's deliberately trying to rankle me. This will not be permissible much longer. She'll learn soon enough.

Allison is performing various calisthenics. She contorts into unspeakable shapes.

"This is no way to conduct yourself," I say as a greeting.

"It's part of my new routine. You know that," she says, panting.

Allison has started a new business on the side. Not kitchen products like Popcorn had hoped. She's developed something along the line of field trips for adults. She stages all kinds of tours in factories, museums, and the like. Allison makes a decent docent, I must admit. Though I wouldn't say that to her face.

Her first tour of a papermill almost extinguished her spirit, however. Everyone walked away from the experience with precisely one bruise each. Allison managed to rally despite the looming thought that more liabilities await her.

"The adult field trip circuit is becoming rather lucrative," Allison says in defense. "If you like money, that is."

She fails at a cartwheel but keeps going. She is both cartwheeling and not. I don't stop her. Erin isn't buying it. Her stare says it all.

Allison cartwheels successfully, but without her initial enthusiasm.

There you have it, folks. This display is simply too much.

"Let me know if you start to feel like you're being held hostage," I say to the turtle on my way to the not-so-secret secret passageway.

Underneath my intricate replica of our town, I've stashed a full stack of Bianca's published diaries for reference. I must finally confirm my theory. I can't surround myself with these distracting shams any longer.

It's wild to think that Bianca's mythology began on the bright, humble stage of her own mind.

I crack open several volumes at once and start flipping pages with abandon. Eventually, I locate the desired entry:

What can I tell you? Who would have thought that a former beauty pageant runner up like me would mingle with an old rodeo clown? He's come a long way since his clowning days. He is soft—like sweatshirt material, not boyfriend material.

In other words, G won't last. G's business partner, C, convinced his wife to make a suicide pact so that C could bail at the last second and not be responsible for her murder. Maybe that's how they handle marriages in a family of former dictators.

When detectives showed up at their mutual place of business to question him, C was able to speed-read one of the detective's notebooks as they took a look around. Whether the notes helped or not remains a mystery, but C has avoided any further line of questioning from the authorities thus far.

How about that. My theory has substance. Victory reverberates through my being at a cellular level.

Time to turn in a complete dossier to my employers. But I'm too emotional to even close this book. And I don't mean that metaphorically. I'm talking about this actual book that Bianca wrote and an imprint of one of the Big Five publishing houses went on to publish.

I could use the kind of plane with a banner trailing behind it. YOUR CUSTOM MESSAGE HERE. Doesn't matter that they're usually advertisements. My employers could look skyward and become one with both nature and theory simultaneously. Can you become one with two ideas at once? Of course you can. You tell 'em I said so. The only downside is that my findings could never fit on such a small banner, even if they're much larger than they look when they're tooling around among the clouds.

How could I begin to divulge that "G" is really Garrett Bruce Lodovico? The Bruce. Our Bruce. His full name confirmed by his own briefcase that was dug up in the lot behind the roller disco a while back, its gold plate engraved with "GBL." Not to mention his obituary. Plus his business partner at the racetrack descended from a Nicaraguan dictator, as we've established. Even though I've never learned his name.

This adds up. I can't really believe it. Am I resting my case?

Erin scoots along the window ledge in the next room. I can see her from the doorway. Allison must've put her up there; there's no way she could get there by herself. Erin stares out over the rooftops and into oblivion. Somebody has to.

24

HALF BAD

WHAT FOLLOWS IS redolent with what feels like a series of mirages.

It's hard to read emotions over email, but once I finagle a rather potent report, my employers seem unenthused and outright stoic about my results.

Most people have a difficult time learning that someone— especially a public figure, celebrity, or symbol of authority—is telling the truth. That life could be both as ordinary and as auspicious as that. Normal can be nauseating to some. Certain folks appear to have an outright aversion to it. I'll admit to feeling a little perturbed that she didn't make it all up. Not even the particulars are invented, from what I can tell.

I guess I've gone back under the radar with no acclaim for my sleuthing. Total crickets.

What was I envisioning anyway? They'd process in a line down our main thoroughfare, disclosing their identities along with their affections? That each in turn would secure a medal around my neck while they're at it? A barbershop quartet could belt out a musical ode to my accomplishments without the world having to end. That could still happen. They're just waiting for a signal from their high priestess or whoever, I'm sure.

To not identify yourself. After all that. But ever since Liz has started cavorting with the historical society like there's not even an ongoing feud between them and the neighborhood watch, she has forced me to accept that she's become a historical society member solely to assume the role of mole. This fusion is murky at best. Some would go so far as to say it's sordid, and it makes me think that an unnatural conglomeration of these two societies actually hired me. These parties know too much. And they're hungry for more. But that's all the resolution I'll ever get in this department. Not everything can be resolved as cleanly as the investigation. I totally nailed it. My Bianca file was nothing short of miraculous.

Would Bianca have hired me all by herself for the boosted publicity? To cement the authentic nature of her work in order to deflate her many critics? If you know, will you tell me?

I take it back.

I can't be trusted.

Bianca has yet to show herself in public since her statue unveiling ceremony. I don't need proof to realize that employment by her would've been all too convenient of a story.

This whole venture is getting old. I burn the town replica in effigy.

With that out of the way, I meet up with the band.

Get this: Reggie is breaking up Rhonda & the Sandwich

Artists. We're done for. At least for now. He's initiating his own solo career. He's been hinting at it since day one of the band. This decision will likely produce his downfall. I don't dare to intervene though. That would only prove futile.

We see him off at the train station. Reggie's gotta stay up. Up and up he goes or you don't want to see the ending. But then again you probably don't want to see the ending either way. This isn't about us. We know that. We have an understanding, Reggie and the rest of us.

Reggie sculpts himself into an affected pose while waiting in line to board the train. He grips his guitar case so tightly I can see his hands changing colors.

"Here goes nothing," Reggie says to himself above the din of fellow passengers.

"What a time to leave. Right when he's risen above his dark past. And just recently elected mayor at that," Vic says.

"Admit it. You all love getting into the thick of situations too," says Laura.

Reggie waves goodbye from what I hypothesize is his seat assignment with his hand out the window. We reciprocate the waving.

"He looks almost regal up there," Vic says.

Let's take another glance. Yup.

Then Reggie tries waving with both hands. His guitar case falls out the window during this cinematic farewell. The instrument flops beneath the tracks. I can almost detect its discordant cry from below as the train chugs out of the station.

We try not to take it as an omen.

"Oh. Hmm. Maybe this means he'll turn around at the next stop and come home," Laura says.

"It's under control!" Reggie's voice wavers out from the window.

25

THE LAST RESORT

THERE'S A KNOCK at our door. I ignore it, assuming it's a delivery for Allison. A parcel filled with one of her many unguents made from ungulates. Something uninteresting no doubt.

Then Allison shouts while I'm climbing the stairs. It's for me. The door's for me.

Bianca is standing here. She sought me out.

Bianca tells me the newest book about her stalker has put her at risk. I read this statement as: It's made her even more famous. When I sit down to read it later on, I'll conclude that her latest book actually does seem fabricated. She changed her mind this time around. She probably got fed up with describing reality.

Anyway, Bianca says she's at risk, blah, blah. She needs more protection than ever before. And she asks me, would I consider being her bodyguard? These words really come out of her mouth.

"More protection?" I say, rapt. "You need a bodyguard?"

"Like you wouldn't believe," she says.

I guess a doberman won't cut it. She needs a visionary. You

would think she'd require something special after her encounters with locals as of late. During the monument unveiling, for example, each townsperson held a torch and formed a fan shape around her statue.

Everyone in the tristate area has tightened security across the board lately, as a matter of fact. The neighborhood watch now requires a code for entry into their meetings and convenes at a different secret location each time. If it wasn't already, our hometown neighborhood watch has officially become an authoritarian regime. There was this one day, I swear I heard them conferring about speed bump placement from down in the sewer. I just happened to be passing by a sewer grate at the right moment and caught a snippet of the conversation.

Back to Bianca. What matters is that she's here, at my doorstep, confiding in me. She's playing to my preternatural sensibilities of stifling overprotection. Surrendering herself to my care. A natural conclusion, you see. However, it's verging on unhelpful, just how protective I am.

I mull her request over. I'm quick at mulling things over though, so it only takes me about three seconds to accept. My best years were spent under fluorescent overhead lights and atop wormy threads of carpeting designed to hide any and every stain. Like the rest of America. Let's try a new pursuit. Bianca could hold an assembly to celebrate my new occupation. There would be much pomp associated with the gesture. Maybe my parents will fly in for the occasion, who knows.

In reality, I speak to no one about this job. Allison is here and loves to eavesdrop, so she doesn't count.

Bianca says I can start immediately. Like, immediately-immediately. I can follow her over to the house and she'll show me how to go about being a bodyguard.

"Is there a packet?" I ask. "An informational packet? For orientation purposes."

"What?"

"Never mind."

I follow her the block and a half that's become so familiar until we arrive at her home. Like I've done so many times before except this time she is fully aware.

This is happening the same day that a new neighbor is moving into Bruce's old house. A single mom with three kids who works in accounting. Of course it doesn't take long to hear from several of the usuals. Within a few hours of her arrival, they claim this lady's a mobster on the side. The only female mob boss in our county. Crunching numbers is a front. We'll see about that.

Bianca and I step over the threshold together. On purpose. To dwell in her dwelling. All appears harmonious at the outset.

Then I see Ryan's set of keys on the entryway table. There's the little hot dog keychain on the loop from his competitive eating days. His essence is all over them. I take the keys as a symbol. He's delivering them over to me. Madonna's "Open Your Heart to Me" starts playing on the jukebox of my mind. At night, I'll hear this song for a week straight on that same jukebox after seeing this.

Bianca stares at his keys.

"Ryan's on another golf trip. He always forgets his keys." "Ah."

"My marriage began with blackmail," is all she can say.

We walk into the living room. Trish is here. She folds a paper twice over and stuffs it down her shirt when she sees us coming. You get the sense something's going on.

There are others peopling the patio. Bianca runs out to greet them. I help myself to the contents of her pantry.

"Don't get too comfortable," Trish says from Bianca's couch.

Trish doesn't prevent me from digging in. She pays no more attention. That much I appreciate.

Bianca pops her head in and tells me, "That'll be enough for now. Thank you."

She returns to her friends on the patio.

"You're right. I don't want to strain myself on the first day," I say to the closed door, but I suppose also to Trish.

Funny enough, this will also be the day Trish runs away with the cheesemonger. We'll have no idea she contained the inclination to rebel against her post beside Bianca.

"Trish was a fetishist," Bianca will say once she's gone, as if that explains everything.

She's always held too many scruples to her name if you ask me. It's common knowledge that every scrupulous person has her unsavory side. Even if Trish had wanted us to believe otherwise for so long before becoming a fugitive.

I return home. Allison offers to train me to get me in the physical shape of a bodyguard. She gives me pointers and shows me the ropes of self defense. She tells me flexibility is more crucial in fighting than people give it credit for. Forget the adult field trips and soothsaying—Allison could be a person trainer if she really wanted to be. But that's the burden of having too many talents. An overwhelming number of options leads to mental paralysis.

Skills are curses too.

Allison calls her training sessions my Appointment with Certain Death. She places a sweatband over my brow, and it feels like she bought it for just this purpose.

Over the next couple of weeks Bianca and I learn that we have nothing to say to each other. I'm here to protect her, not to become the last great conversationalist. I start drumming my fingers on countertops, tables, all surfaces, as a compensatory tic. To fill the space. All while monitoring the scene. Scanning for dangers. Patrolling for potential threats. I'm not a drummer by any stretch. Never touched a cymbal. A high hat does seem especially festive. But I will continue to do this amid the incalculable minutes of silence alone with Bianca. To the point that she'll presume I'm a serious drummer. That it's my instrument in our now-defunct band. Laura would laugh at me. If only she could see me now.

Bianca doesn't know how hard I'm working. Nobody does. I devote myself to fresh orders every weekday. I lead her to believe there's not much to it. I'm an effortless bodyguard. At least I can know who she is, who really employs me, unlike last time. After all those diary entries, you could say I know her a little too well. And she gives me performance reviews, so I don't have to guess what she really thinks about my work either.

I'm learning the tricks of the trade. I'm not learning anything at all.

As for Trish, she and the cheesemonger are in another hemisphere. I have her number somehow, so I text her: I hope you get everything that's coming to you. I'll leave her to interpret my message in either a positive or negative direction. Whichever suits her mood. If her phone still works.

Bianca and I will probably hit our stride, but it hasn't happened so far. We're in the realm of accomplices for now. A pretend friend. I relish all the crimes of pretend friendship I have yet to commit. Don't hold back. You know I won't.

We don't talk about my previous assignment or the stalker or the closed investigation whatsoever. I'll never fess up to any of it. I can maintain confidentiality, people. Right to the end.

THE END